Usborne Spotter's Guides
THE
NIGHT SKY

Nigel Henbest MSc FRAS
and Stuart Atkinson

D0413001

Edited by Philippa Wingate
Designed by Nickey Butler
Cover designer: Michael Hill
Series designer: Laura Fearn

This edition first published in 2006 by Usborne Publishing Ltd.,
Usborne House, 83-85 Saffron Hill, London, EC1N 8RT,
England. www.usborne.com

Printed in China

CONTENTS

This photograph shows the surface of Earth's Moon

HOW TO USE THIS BOOK

This book is an identification guide to the things you can see in the night sky. Take it with you when you go out spotting. Over a period of about a year, you should be able to see most of the things in this book that are visible from where you live.

WHAT TO LOOK FOR

You can find out which constellations will be visible using the sky map on page 10 (or page 12 if you live in the southern hemisphere). Look to see where the planets will be (pages 38-42), and find out about comets and asteroids (pages 44 and 45).

NEAR AND FAR

Some objects, like the stars, are very distant, while the planets, comets and the Moon are much closer. This book starts with the distant sky sights, then moves to ones closer to Earth, with descriptions to help you identify them.

MAKE YOUR MARK

Next to most of the things in the book is a circle. Whenever you spot an object, make a mark in the circle. Some things, like the more distant planets, can only be seen using extremely powerful telescopes, so these don't have circles next to them.

There is a scorecard at the back of the book. Give yourself a score for each of the things you see.

	Score	Date spotted
Carina (S)	10	12/07
Cassiopeia (N)	5	
Centaurus (S)	5	09/10
Cepheus (N)	15	01/06
Cetus (N)	15	
Chameleon (S)	20	03/03

The letter N or S next to an object indicates that it is visible only in the northern or southern hemisphere

Planet Earth photographed from space

OUT SPOTTING

When you go out spotting, make sure you are well prepared. This section tells you what you'll need.

WHAT TO TAKE
• this book

• warm clothing, because you'll get cold when sitting still, even in summer

• a flashlight for looking at the star maps in this book

• binoculars or a telescope

• a notebook and pencil to record what you see

• a chair or mat to sit on, as standing up soon becomes uncomfortable.

IN THE DARK
Your eyes will take about 20 minutes to adapt to the darkness, so wait for a while before you try to spot the fainter stars. Use your flashlight to read the star maps in this book. The flashlight's glare can keep you from seeing well in the dark, so take care not to look directly at the light.

TAKE CARE
Don't go out in the dark alone. Go with a parent or guardian, or members of your astronomy club. (Visit **www.usborne-quicklinks.com** for details of clubs and organizations.)

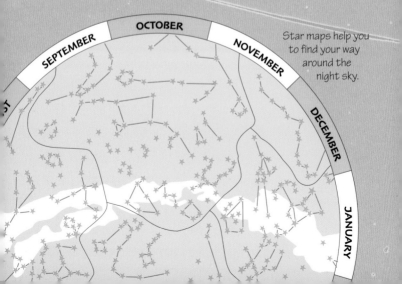

Star maps help you to find your way around the night sky.

Eyepiece   Focusing
              control

Lightweight
binoculars are
easier to hold
still than big,
heavy ones.

BINOCULARS

You can see most of the
sights in this book with
your unaided eyes, but
you'll see much more
with a pair of binoculars.

Visit a good shop and
try out several pairs. A
pair of 7x50 binoculars
are ideal for looking at
the stars. Don't buy a
pair more than 10x50
or they will be too heavy.

TELESCOPES

Telescopes are more
powerful than binoculars,
but more expensive.
Many of the cheaper
ones are not very good.
For the cost of a cheap
telescope, it's better
to buy a good pair
of binoculars.

Eyepiece

Your telescope will need a
mount. Without one, you
will not be able to hold the
telescope still enough to
see anything.

7

This photo shows
the Sun's endlessly
churning surface.

THE UNIVERSE

The Universe is the name
given to the collection
of all things that exist in
space. It's made up of
millions of stars, planets,
and vast clouds of gas.

LIGHT YEARS

Distances in space are
huge, so astronomers
measure them in light
years. One light year (LY)
is the distance light travels
in a year – 9.46 million
million* km (5.88 million
million* miles). Light travels
at a speed of 300,000km
(186,000 miles) per second.

GALAXIES

Vast groups of stars are
called galaxies. Earth is
in the Milky Way galaxy.
Astronomers think it
contains about
100,000 million stars.

The Milky Way is a vast,
spiral-shaped galaxy.

THE SUN

A star is a ball of hot gas
which produces heat
and light from a nuclear
reaction within its core.
The closest star to Earth is
the Sun. After the Sun the
nearest star is Proxima
Centauri, 4.3 LY away.

THE EARTH

The Earth is one of nine
planets which orbit (go
around) the Sun. Together,
the Sun and everything
that orbits it are called
the Solar System. The Earth
takes one year to orbit
the Sun. As it orbits, it
spins, making a complete
spin once a day.

* Trillion in the USA

For a link to a fun space website with activities, turn to page 54.

SATELLITES

Any object in space that orbits around another is called a satellite. The Moon is a satellite that orbits the Earth once every 27.3 days. It is the Earth's only natural satellite. Most of the other planets have natural satellites.

THE BIG BANG

Many scientists think the Universe began about 15,000 million years ago in an enormous explosion, known as the Big Bang. Gas clouds thrown out by the explosion turned into galaxies. Even today, the galaxies are racing apart from each other as a result of the explosion.

THE BIG BANG THEORY

The Big Bang created a huge fireball. As this cooled, it began to spread out.

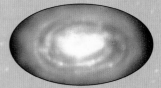

Thick clouds of gases began to form into vast, dense clumps of matter.

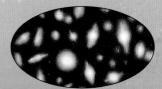

Stars and galaxies were gradually formed from this matter.

9

STARS OF THE NORTHERN SKIES

On a clear night you can
see about 3,000 stars in the
sky. Astronomers find their way
around by grouping the stars into
patterns, called constellations.

The best time to use the star
map is around 11:00pm.
Spotting some of the
constellations can be
tricky. It is best to choose
a dark place on a dark,
clear night.

USING THE STAR MAP

Turn the book around
until the current month
is nearest to you. Face
south and look for the
stars as they appear on
the map. You should be
able to see most of the
stars in the middle and
lower part of the map.

When you have found the
constellations shown here, turn
to the larger-scale maps on the
following pages. The black lines
on this map show the areas
covered by each double-page.
The page numbers to look up
are marked in each section.

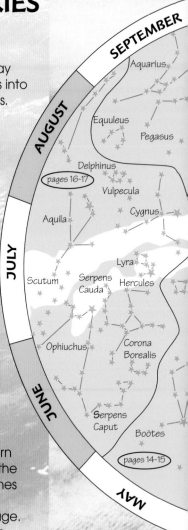

SEPTEMBER

AUGUST

JULY

JUNE

MAY

Aquarius

Equuleus

Pegasus

Delphinus

pages 16-17

Vulpecula

Cygnus

Aquila

Lyra

Scutum

Serpens
Cauda

Hercules

Ophiuchus

Corona
Borealis

Serpens
Caput

Boötes

pages 14-15

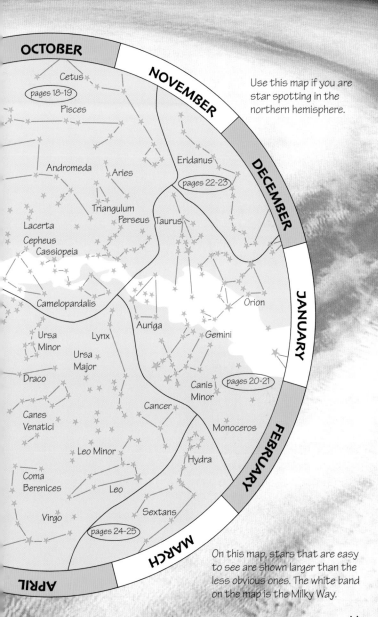

OCTOBER

NOVEMBER

DECEMBER

JANUARY

FEBRUARY

MARCH

APRIL

Cetus

pages 18-19

Pisces

Andromeda

Aries

Eridanus

pages 22-23

Triangulum

Perseus

Taurus

Lacerta

Cepheus

Cassiopeia

Camelopardalis

Orion

Auriga

Gemini

Ursa
Minor

Lynx

Ursa
Major

Draco

Canis
Minor

pages 20-21

Canes
Venatici

Cancer

Monoceros

Leo Minor

Hydra

Coma
Berenices

Leo

Virgo

Sextans

pages 24-25

Use this map if you are
star spotting in the
northern hemisphere.

On this map, stars that are easy
to see are shown larger than the
less obvious ones. The white band
on the map is the Milky Way.

11

For a link to a site that includes an interactive star map, turn to page 54.

STARS OF THE SOUTHERN SKIES

If you live in the southern hemisphere, use this map to find your way around the skies.

Turn the map until the current month is nearest you. Face north, and you should be able to see most of the stars shown in the middle and lower part of the map.

When you look at Sagittarius, you are also looking toward the middle of the Milky Way galaxy, so you will see lots of stars in that area of the sky. To the south you can see the Southern Cross, Crux.

When you have found the constellations shown here, turn to the larger-scale maps on the following pages. The black lines on this map show the areas covered by each double-page. The page numbers to look up are marked in each section.

The maps on the following pages only show the approximate positions of stars and galaxies.

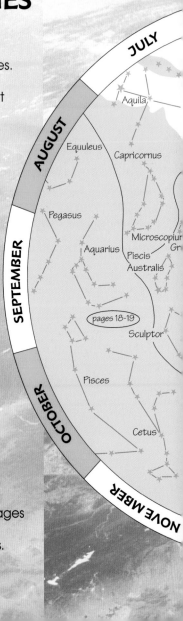

JULY

AUGUST

SEPTEMBER

OCTOBER

NOVEMBER

Aquila

Equuleus

Capricornus

Pegasus

Microscopiur

Aquarius

Piscis

Gr

Australis

pages 18-19

Sculptor

Pisces

Cetus

JUNE

MAY

Use this map if you are
star spotting in the
southern hemisphere.

Ophiuchus

pages 16-17

Serpens
Caput

Scutum

pages 14-15

APRIL

Sagittarius

Scorpius

Libra

Virgo

pages 26-27

Telescopium

Norma

Lupus

Ara

Centaurus

Corona
Australis

Triangulum
Austale

Circinus

Corvus

Indus

Musca

Crux

Crater

MARCH

Apus

Chameleon

Pavo

Octans

Sextans

Tucana

Hydrus

Antlia

Mensa

Volans

Vela

Horologium

Carina

Pyxis

Hydra

enix

Reticulum

Pictor

Puppis

pages 24-25

Dorado

Columba

Canis
Major

FEBRUARY

Fornax

Caelum

Monoceros

Lepus

Eridanus

pages 20-21

pages 22-23

JANUARY

Orion

DECEMBER

The size of each star symbol
shows how bright the star
is, not its actual size.

13

For a link to a new astronomy picture every day, turn to page 54.

DRACO TO CANCER

○ 1 DRACO (DRAGON)
A long, straggling line
of faint stars. Its "head"
is a group of four stars
near Vega; the "tail"
loops around Ursa Minor
(see no. 6 below).

**○ 2 CANES VENATICI
(HUNTING DOGS)**
This constellation was named in
1650. The "dogs" hunt the "bears",
following them across the sky.

○ 3 BOÖTES (HERDSMAN)
A kite shape. Arcturus is the
fourth brightest star in the
sky. Find it using the curved
handle of the Plough* (see
no.8 below) as a pointer.

**○ 4 COMA BERENICES
(BERENICE'S HAIR)**
A cloud of faint stars.
Binoculars will show
about 30 of them.

○ 5 VIRGO (VIRGIN)
A constellation
representing the
goddess of justice.
Spica is a hot,
bright white star.

**○ 6 URSA MINOR
(LITTLE BEAR)**
Polaris, the pole
star, is important to
navigators because
it is always due north.

○ 7 LYNX
A line of faint stars.
Very hard to see.

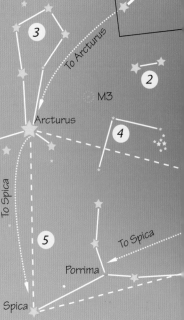

Vega links to the
map on page 17.

1

Nu
Draconis

6

Kocab

Thuban

The Plough*

Alcor and Mizar

3

To Arcturus

2

M3

Arcturus

4

To Spica

To Spica

5

Porrima

Spica

* Big Dipper in the USA

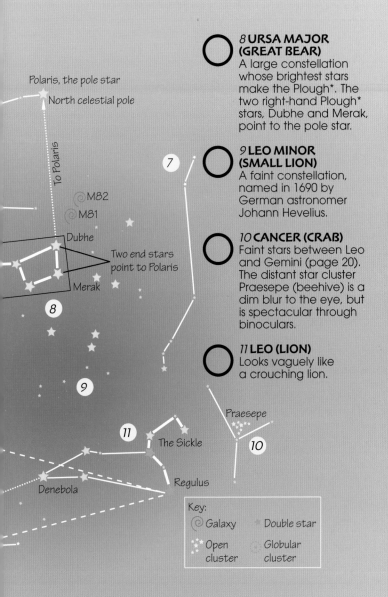

Polaris, the pole star

North celestial pole

To Polaris

M82
M81

Dubhe

Two end stars
point to Polaris

Merak

8

9

7

8 URSA MAJOR (GREAT BEAR)
A large constellation whose brightest stars make the Plough*. The two right-hand Plough* stars, Dubhe and Merak, point to the pole star.

9 LEO MINOR (SMALL LION)
A faint constellation, named in 1690 by German astronomer Johann Hevelius.

10 CANCER (CRAB)
Faint stars between Leo and Gemini (page 20). The distant star cluster Praesepe (beehive) is a dim blur to the eye, but is spectacular through binoculars.

11 LEO (LION)
Looks vaguely like a crouching lion.

Praesepe

11

The Sickle

10

Regulus

Denebola

Key:
- Galaxy
- Double star
- Open cluster
- Globular cluster

CYGNUS TO SERPENS

12 CYGNUS (SWAN)
The bright star Deneb forms one corner of the Summer Triangle, together with Vega and Altair. Binoculars show many faint stars in Cygnus.

13 DELPHINUS (DOLPHIN)
A compact constellation with a very distinctive shape. Delphinus' "tail" star is 950 LY away.

14 SAGITTA (ARROW)
Four stars make an arrow shape, between Cygnus and Aquila. This constellation is very faint, and isn't shown on the map.

15 CAPRICORNUS (GOAT)
A distorted triangle of faint stars. Giedi is a double star. The planet Neptune was in Capricornus when first discovered.

16 AQUILA (EAGLE)
The bright star Altair is easily recognized because of its two fainter flanking stars.

17 SCUTUM (SHIELD)
Faint constellation, visible against the Milky Way.

18 VULPECULA (FOX)
A very inconspicuous star group. Originally called the fox and goose.

Key:
- Nebula
- Open cluster
- Galaxy
- Double star
- Globular cluster
- Planetary nebula

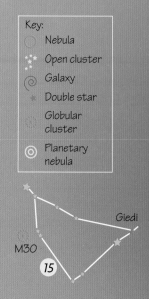

Giedi

M30

15

19 LYRA (LYRE)
A small but easily spotted group. Vega is the fifth brightest star in the sky, 26 LY away.

20 OPHIUCHUS (SERPENT BEARER)
A very large group of stars forming a distorted circle.

21 HERCULES
A large constellation, but rather shapeless and difficult to recognize.

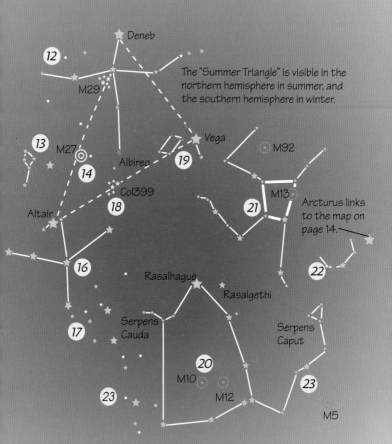

Deneb

12

M29

The "Summer Triangle" is visible in the northern hemisphere in summer, and the southern hemisphere in winter.

13

M27

14

Albireo

19

Vega

M92

M13

21

Arcturus links to the map on page 14.

Col399

18

Altair

16

22

Rasalhague

Rasalgethi

17

Serpens Cauda

Serpens Caput

20

23

M10

M12

23

M5

M62

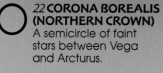

22 CORONA BOREALIS (NORTHERN CROWN)
A semicircle of faint stars between Vega and Arcturus.

23 SERPENS (SERPENT)
Consists of two separate parts: Caput (head) and Cauda (tail) lying either side of Ophiuchus.

Antares links to the map on page 27. This star appears in Scorpius.

CAMELOPARDALIS TO AQUARIUS

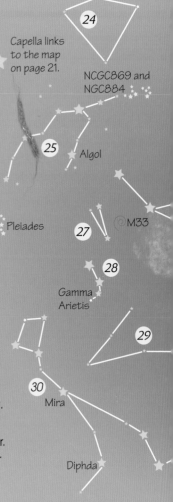

⭕ **24 CAMELOPARDALIS (GIRAFFE)**
Hard to see these stars with the naked eye.

⭕ **25 PERSEUS**
Named after a Greek hero. Algol is two stars close together.

⭕ **26 ANDROMEDA**
Named after a mythical princess. This galaxy can be seen with the naked eye even though it is over 2 million LY away.

⭕ **27 TRIANGULUM (TRIANGLE)**
A compact pattern of three faint stars.

⭕ **28 ARIES (RAM)**
Three main stars. Gamma Arietis is a double star.

⭕ **29 PISCES (FISHES)**
In myth, two fish tied together by a long ribbon.

⭕ **30 CETUS (WHALE)**
Mira is a red star in Cetus. It remains visible to the naked eye for six months of the year, then fades to invisibility.

⭕ **31 CEPHEUS**
In myth, Andromeda's father. Its brightest star is Alderamin.

⭕ **32 LACERTA (LIZARD)**
A zig-zag of very faint stars. It is hard to find.

Capella links to the map on page 21.

NCGC869 and NGC884

Algol

Pleiades

M33

Gamma Arietis

Mira

Diphda

18

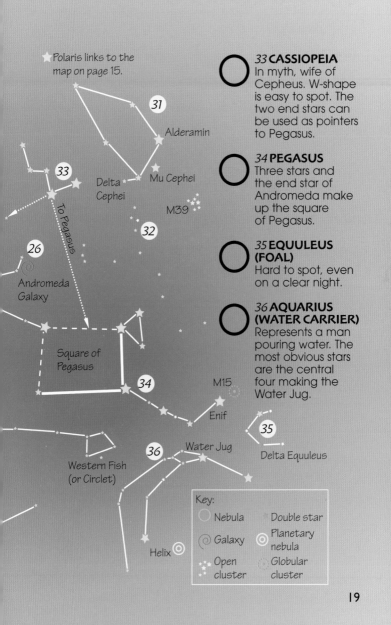

Polaris links to the map on page 15.

31

Alderamin

33

Delta Cephei

Mu Cephei

M39

32

26

Andromeda Galaxy

To Pegasus

Square of Pegasus

34

M15

Enif

35

Water Jug

Delta Equuleus

Western Fish (or Circlet)

36

Helix ⊙

33 CASSIOPEIA
In myth, wife of Cepheus. W-shape is easy to spot. The two end stars can be used as pointers to Pegasus.

34 PEGASUS
Three stars and the end star of Andromeda make up the square of Pegasus.

35 EQUULEUS (FOAL)
Hard to spot, even on a clear night.

36 AQUARIUS (WATER CARRIER)
Represents a man pouring water. The most obvious stars are the central four making the Water Jug.

Key:
- ◯ Nebula
- ◎ Galaxy
- ∴ Open cluster
- ✦ Double star
- ◉ Planetary nebula
- ⦿ Globular cluster

19

GEMINI TO LEPUS

37 GEMINI (TWINS)
Castor is actually six stars very close together, but binoculars cannot separate them. The faint planets Uranus and Pluto were in Gemini when discovered.

38 CANIS MINOR (SMALL DOG)
In myth, the smaller of the two dogs of Orion the hunter. Procyon is the eighth brightest star in the sky, and at 11 LY, one of the closest to Earth.

39 MONOCEROS (UNICORN)
Inconspicuous and given its name in the 17th century, but worth "sweeping" with your binoculars for star clusters and nebulae.

40 CANIS MAJOR (LARGE DOG)
A compact group of bright stars. Sirius (the Dog Star) is the brightest star in the sky. Read more about it on page 31.

41 AURIGA (CHARIOTEER)
A curving line of stars ending in a distinct but faint triangle known as the Kids. Capella is the sixth brightest star in the sky and 42 LY from Earth.

Castor

The Twins

Pollux

37

Delta Gemini

Rosette Nebula

38

Procyon

NGC2244

The Winter Triangle

39

Lots of star clusters in this area

Sirius

40

M41

Adara

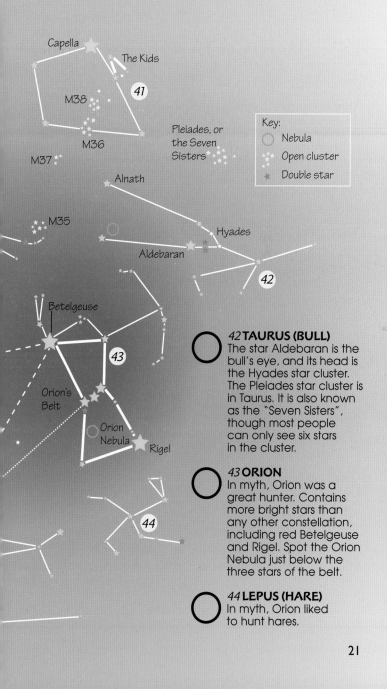

Key:
- ◯ Nebula
- ✦ Open cluster
- ✦ Double star

42 TAURUS (BULL)
The star Aldebaran is the bull's eye, and its head is the Hyades star cluster. The Pleiades star cluster is in Taurus. It is also known as the "Seven Sisters", though most people can only see six stars in the cluster.

43 ORION
In myth, Orion was a great hunter. Contains more bright stars than any other constellation, including red Betelgeuse and Rigel. Spot the Orion Nebula just below the three stars of the belt.

44 LEPUS (HARE)
In myth, Orion liked to hunt hares.

COLUMBA TO MICROSCOPIUM

45 COLUMBA (DOVE)
A distinct group of stars lying near Canopus, named in 1679.

This is the lower part of Orion, and links to the map on page 21.

Rigel

46 HOROLOGIUM (PENDULUM CLOCK)
Only one star is easily visible in this constellation.

47 CAELUM (CHISEL)
Consists of a few very faint stars.

48 RETICULUM (NET)
A distinct little group of faint stars between Canopus and Achernar.

49 MENSA (TABLE MOUNTAIN)
The faintest constellation in the sky. Look for it on a very clear night.

50 HYDRUS (SMALL WATER SNAKE)
A large triangle lying between the misty patches of the Magellanic Clouds.

51 OCTANS (OCTANT)
Always due south, but has no bright star to match Polaris in the northern hemisphere.

52 PAVO (PEACOCK)
Conspicuous group of faint stars. Kappa Pavonis is a variable star, changing from dim to bright and back again every 19 days.

53 INDUS (INDIAN)
Lies between Pavo and Grus.

54 FORNAX (FURNACE)
Lies in a curve of Eridanus.

55 TUCANA (TOUCAN)
A group of faint stars, named in 1603 by Johann Bayer.

45

56 ERIDANUS (RIVER ERIDANUS)
A winding line of stars, named after a mythological river. It ends at Achernar, the ninth brightest star in the sky.

57 PHOENIX
Named in 1603 after the mythological bird which rises from its own ashes.

58 SCULPTOR
Consists of very faint stars. It was first called the sculptor's workshop.

59 PISCIS AUSTRINUS (SOUTHERN FISH)
Includes the star Fomalhaut, which is 24 LY from Earth.

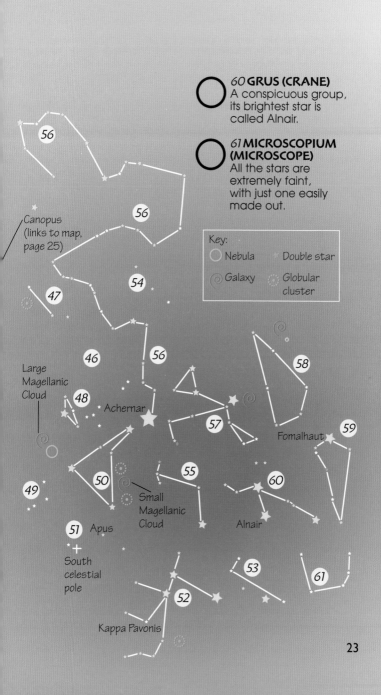

60 GRUS (CRANE)
A conspicuous group, its brightest star is called Alnair.

61 MICROSCOPIUM (MICROSCOPE)
All the stars are extremely faint, with just one easily made out.

Key:
⬤ Nebula   ✳ Double star
◎ Galaxy   ⦿ Globular cluster

Canopus (links to map, page 25)

Large Magellanic Cloud

Achernar

Small Magellanic Cloud

Apus

South celestial pole

Fomalhaut

Alnair

Kappa Pavonis

23

CORVUS TO DORADO

Spica links to the map on page 14.

○ **62 CORVUS (CROW)**
A distinct foursome of stars in a rather barren area of the sky.

○ **63 CRATER (CUP)**
Another group of four stars, like a fainter Corvus.

M83: Galaxy in Hydra

○ **64 ANTLIA (AIR PUMP)**
A triangle of faint stars, named in 1763.

This area is full of clusters and nebulae

○ **65 VELA (SAIL)**
Part of the ancient constellation of the ship of Argo. Carina and Puppis form the rest. Its outline is marked by bright stars; binoculars show fainter ones.

The constellation Crux, often called the Southern Cross, links to the map on page 27.

○ **66 CHAMELEON**
Four faint stars.

○ **67 VOLANS (FLYING FISH)**
A distinct group of faint stars, partly enclosed by Carina.

○ **70 PYXIS (COMPASS)**
A few faint stars between Vela and Puppis.

○ **71 PUPPIS (STERN)**
Another part of Argo, the ship in Jason's quest for the Golden Fleece. Many stars and nebulae are visible through binoculars.

○ **68 SEXTANS (SEXTANT)**
A small group of faint stars between Leo and Hydra.

○ **69 HYDRA (WATER SNAKE)**
The longest constellation in the sky. The "head" is a conspicuous small group of six stars. The constellation only contains one bright star, Alphard.

○ **72 CARINA (KEEL)**
A line of stars forming the bottom of the ship Argo. At one end is Canopus, 120 LY distant and the second brightest star in the sky.

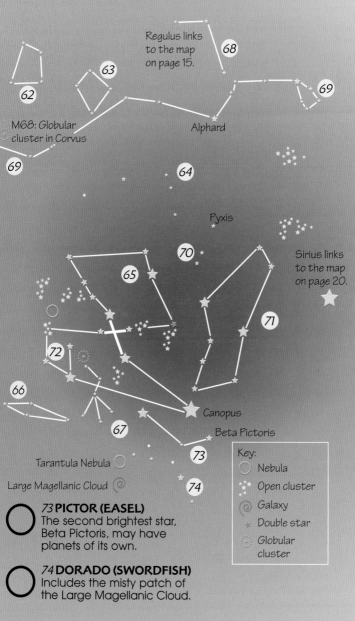

Regulus links
to the map
on page 15.

68

63

62

69

M68: Globular
cluster in Corvus

Alphard

69

64

Pyxis

70

Sirius links
to the map
on page 20.

65

71

72

66

67

Canopus

Beta Pictoris

73

Tarantula Nebula

Large Magellanic Cloud

74

Key:
○ Nebula
✳ Open cluster
◎ Galaxy
✦ Double star
⬚ Globular
cluster

○ 73 PICTOR (EASEL)
The second brightest star,
Beta Pictoris, may have
planets of its own.

○ 74 DORADO (SWORDFISH)
Includes the misty patch of
the Large Magellanic Cloud.

25

SAGITTARIUS TO CRUX

75 SAGITTARIUS (ARCHER)
A distinctive "teapot" shape of bright stars. The misty nebula M8 is a region where stars are forming.

76 CORONA AUSTRALIS (SOUTHERN CROWN)
Faint stars in a curving group of stars.

77 TELESCOPIUM (TELESCOPE)
A group of faint stars near the tail of Scorpius.

78 ARA (ALTAR)
Lies between Alpha Centauri and the tail of Scorpius.

79 CIRCINUS (COMPASSES)
Consists of three faint stars near Alpha Centauri. Named in the 18th century.

80 TRIANGULUM AUSTRALE (SOUTHERN TRIANGLE)
An easily spotted triangle of bright stars, named in 1603. The brightest star is only 100 LY away.

81 APUS (BIRD OF PARADISE)
An inconspicuous group of stars, named in 1603.

82 MUSCA (FLY)
A group of faint stars next to the Southern Cross.

83 SCORPIUS (SCORPION)
Bright stars outline a realistic scorpion shape. Antares is a very bright red star. Binoculars show many faint star clusters.

84 LIBRA (SCALES)
Four faint stars form the main part of Libra.

85 LUPUS (WOLF)
A distinctive pattern of bright stars, stretching from Alpha Centauri to Antares.

86 NORMA (LEVEL)
A group of faint stars. The region is filled with star clusters, since part of Norma lies in the Milky Way.

87 CENTAURUS (CENTAUR)
In myth, a centaur was a creature half-man, half-horse. Alpha Centauri is the third brightest star in the sky.

88 CRUX (SOUTHERN CROSS)
Alpha and Gamma Crucis point to the south celestial pole (the point directly above the south pole on Earth).

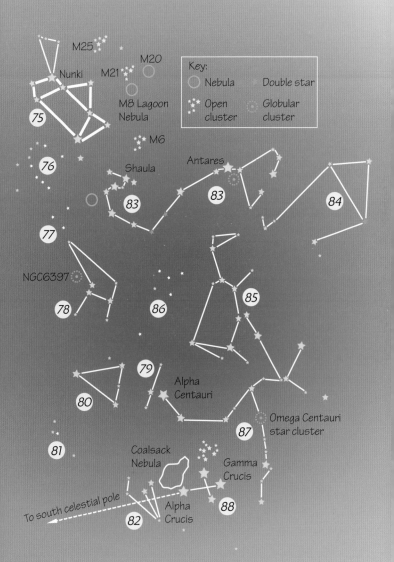

M25

Nunki

M21

M20

M8 Lagoon
Nebula

Key:
Nebula   Double star
Open   Globular
cluster   cluster

75

M6

76

Shaula   Antares

77   83   83   84

NGC6397

78   86   85

79

80   Alpha
            Centauri

81   Omega Centauri
                        star cluster

87

Coalsack   Gamma
Nebula   Crucis

To south celestial pole   Alpha   88
                            Crucis

82

27

BIRTH OF STARS

New stars form inside huge clouds of swirling dust and gas called nebulae. Within them, nuclear reactions begin, and a new star is formed. At the core of a star like the Sun, the temperature is about 15 million $^{\circ}$C (27 million $^{\circ}$F).

These pages show some nebulae and star clusters. There are millions more, but the ones shown are visible as faint, fuzzy patches to the naked eye. Some star clusters stay together, but many break up. The stars may end up single, like the Sun.

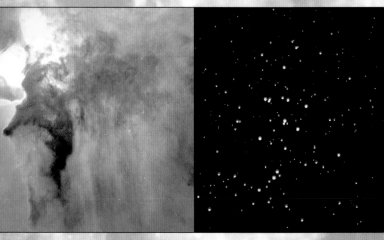

↑LAGOON NEBULA (page 27)
Large clouds made of hydrogen gas. The star which makes the gas glow is so deeply embedded in dust that it cannot be seen. This nebula is over 5,000 LY away.

↑PRAESEPE (page 15)
An easily spotted cluster, 40 LY across and about 525 LY from Earth. Most of the stars (about 200) are thought to be about 400 million years old. No glowing nebula of hydrogen gas is visible.

More often, the stars end up in a pair or a trio.

A number of new stars that are still close together is called an open cluster. Globular clusters look like a single faint star, but are made up of up to a million stars.

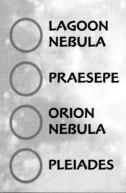

○ **LAGOON NEBULA**

○ **PRAESEPE**

○ **ORION NEBULA**

○ **PLEIADES**

↑ORION NEBULA (page 21)
This is a huge glowing cloud of gas. It can be seen clearly with the naked eye, from both the northern and southern hemisphere, in the middle of Orion. It is 5,700 LY from Earth.

↑PLEIADES (page 21)
This star cluster is made up of over 250 stars, and was formed about 60 million years ago. It is often called the Seven Sisters, though only six bright stars are visible to the naked eye.

TYPES OF STARS

Stars vary enormously in size, shade and temperature. New stars tend to burn bright and hot. They look blue or white. Older stars are cooler and shine less brightly, and can look orange or red.

At 5,000 million years old, our Sun is a "middle-aged" star. Stars the size of our Sun have a lifespan of about 10,000 million years. Smaller stars, called dwarf stars, live longer.

Stars that are larger than our Sun are called giant stars. The biggest are called supergiant stars. They live for only a few million years.

This chart shows the shades and temperatures of some typical stars.

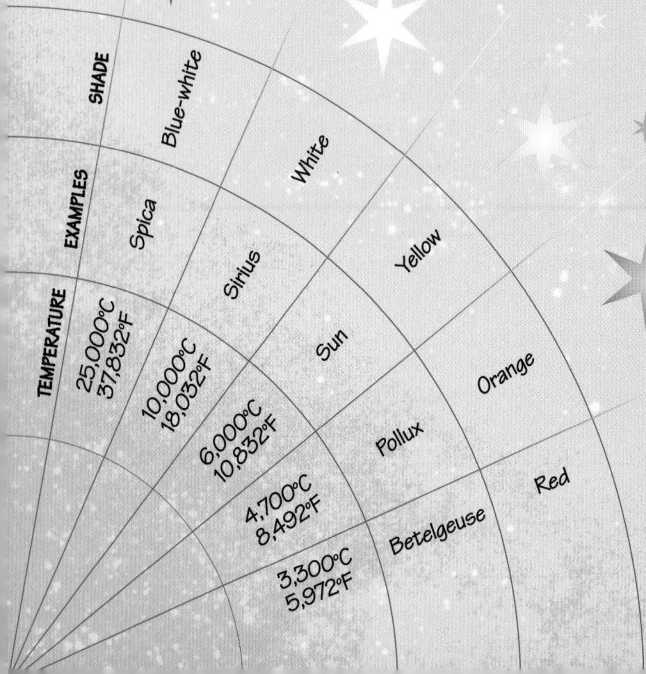

SHADE	EXAMPLES	TEMPERATURE
Blue-white	Spica	25,000°C 37,832°F
White	Sirius	10,000°C 18,032°F
Yellow	Sun	6,000°C 10,832°F
Orange	Pollux	4,700°C 8,492°F
Red	Betelgeuse	3,300°C 5,972°F

* Big Dipper in the USA

➡ ALGOL (page 18)

Algol is a variable star. Every three days, it dims for ten hours, but not because its light output changes. It is in fact a double star, and one of the pair periodically blocks off the light of the other, reducing the brightness. About half of all known stars occur in pairs like this.

⬅ SIRIUS (page 20)

Sirius, 8.6 LY from Earth, has a faint companion which is a white dwarf. You can't see the dwarf, but should have no problem finding Sirius. Sirius is known as the "Dog Star" as it is in Canis Major. It's the brightest star in the sky.

➡ MIZAR AND ALCOR (page 14)

Mizar, the second star in the "handle" of the Plough*, has a companion star, Alcor, which can be spotted with the naked eye. Mizar itself is a double star, but the pair can only be seen with a telescope.

Alcor ➡   ⬅Mizar

For a link to a site where you can watch space videos, turn to page 54.

DYING STARS

Stars don't shine forever. Eventually their supply of gas runs out and they die. As they die, stars that are the size of our Sun (or smaller) swell up and turn red. They are then called red giants. Slowly they puff their outer layers of gas into space.

A small, almost dead star, called a white dwarf is left. It eventually cools and fades.

Stars that are bigger than our Sun have a spectacular death. They swell up into vast red stars known as red supergiants. Then they blow up with a huge explosion called a supernova.

Barnard's Star is a dwarf star, cooler than our Sun.

The Sun is a yellow star.

This diagram compares the size of some bright stars, including our Sun.

Arcturus is in the constellation of Boötes (see page 14). It is a giant star.

Rigel, in the constellation of Orion (see page 21) is a supergiant star.

➡ BETELGEUSE (page 21)

A red giant, easily spotted at the "shoulder" of Orion. The star varies in brightness slowly. Its size varies with its brightness. At its maximum, it is nearly 700 million km (438 million miles) across, over 500 times as large as the Sun.

⬅ ANTARES (page 26)

Another old red giant, about 400 million km (250 million miles) in diameter. It has a small companion star which can only be seen with a telescope. The companion is greenish. Antares' surface temperature is only 3,300°C (5,972°F)

➡ MIRA (page 18)

The central star in the constellation of Cetus is a red giant whose brightness varies. Over months its brightness can increase about a thousand times.

GALAXIES

The stars you see in the sky are part of a spiral group of 100,000 million stars, called the Milky Way galaxy. You can see only a fraction of these stars.

Beyond the Milky Way are billions more galaxies. The light from the distant galaxies blends together to form a misty band stretching across the sky which passes through the constellations of Cygnus, Cassiopeia, Aquila, Vela, Sagittarius, Scorpius, Centaurus, Crux, Puppis, Monoceros and Perseus.

◀ MILKY WAY

This is a section of the Milky Way as seen through a telescope. Using binoculars, you may see faint nebulae and star clusters within it.

Dust particles in space absorb starlight, producing dark "holes" in the Milky Way. Look in the constellation of Orion for the Horse's Head Nebula shown here.

For a link to pictures from the Hubble Space Telescope, turn to page 54.

➡ ANDROMEDA GALAXY (page 19)

To the naked eye it looks like a faint blur. It is almost 2.2 million LY away and is the most distant object you can see without binoculars or a telescope. Its spiral shape is similar to that of the Milky Way. Galaxies group together in clusters. Andromeda is a member of the Local Group, along with the Milky Way, the Magellanic Clouds and about 25 other galaxies.

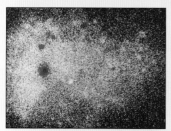

Large Magellanic Cloud

Small Magellanic Cloud

⬅ MAGELLANIC CLOUDS (pages 23, 25)

These bright, misty patches, visible only from the southern hemisphere, were first spotted by the explorer Ferdinand Magellan in 1521. They are smaller than our galaxy. Neither of the clouds has a distinctive shape, which is unusual, because galaxies usually have a spiral or oval shape.

35

EMPIRE OF THE SUN

On a clear night you'll probably see one or more bright points of light that aren't marked on the star maps. These are planets.

All the planets revolve around the Sun in the same direction. They gradually change their positions against the background stars, so they can't be marked on the constellation maps. After each planet's description on the following pages, there is a table that tells you where and when to

The Solar System. The planets and the distances between them are not shown to scale.

Sun

Mercury

Venus

Earth

Mars

Jupiter

PLANETARY FACT-FINDER

PLANET	NUMBER OF MOONS	AVERAGE DISTANCE FROM THE SUN
Mercury	None	58 million km (36 million miles)
Venus	None	108 million km (68 million miles)
Earth	1	149 million km (93 million miles)
Mars	2	228 million km (143 million miles)
Jupiter	At least 61	778 million km (486 million miles)
Saturn	At least 34	1,429 million km (893 million miles)
Uranus	At least 27	2,875 million km (1,797 million miles)
Neptune	At least 13	4,500 million km (2,813 million miles)
Pluto	1	5,900 million km (3,688 million miles)

For a link to a fly-through of a Virtual Solar System, turn to page 54.

look for the planets during the next few years. The planets seem to move through the same groups of constellations, known as the zodiac. The zodiac consists of Pisces, Aries, Taurus, Gemini, Cancer, Leo, Virgo, Scorpius, Sagittarius, Capricornus, Libra and Aquarius.

Apart from Uranus, Neptune and Pluto, the planets appear very bright. Once you have located their constellations you can't miss them.

Saturn

Uranus

Pluto

Neptune

DIAMETER	TIME TO ORBIT SUN (A YEAR)	TIME TO SPIN ONCE (A DAY)
4,880km (3,050 miles)	88 days	59 days
12,104km (7,565 miles)	225 days	243 days
12,756km (7,972 miles)	365.3 days	23hrs 56 mins
6,794km (4,246 miles)	687 days	24hrs 37 mins
142,984km (89,365 miles)	11.9 years	9hrs 50 mins
120,536km (75,335 miles)	29.5 years	10hrs 14 mins
51,158km (31,974 miles)	84 years	17hrs 14 mins
49,532km (30,958 miles)	165 years	18hrs
2,274km (1,421 miles)	248 years	6 days 10hrs

Mercury can only be seen low on the horizon in the twilight glow.

MERCURY

The diameter of Mercury, the closest planet to the Sun, is only 50% larger than that of the Moon. It has no atmosphere and during its day, the Sun bakes its surface up to 427°C (800°F). At night, its temperature can fall to –183°C (–300°F). Mercury is heavily cratered like the Moon, and has long ridges where it has shrunk slightly, like an old apple.

MERCURY - WHEN AND WHERE TO LOOK

YEAR	MORNING SKY	EVENING SKY
2006	August; November-December	February-March; May-June
2007	March; October-November	January-February; May-June
2008	March; October-November	January; April-May
2009	February; September-October	January; April-May; December
2010	January-February; September-October	March-April; November-December

VENUS

Venus is a similar size to the Earth, but its atmosphere is a hundred times thicker and made of choking carbon dioxide. This thick blanket makes Venus' surface very hot – about 480°C (900°F). The planet is veiled by clouds made of acid droplets. Space probes have shown that its surface has craters, mountains and valleys.

VENUS – WHEN AND WHERE TO LOOK

YEAR	MORNING SKY	EVENING SKY
2006	February–September	January; December
2007	January–August	September–December
2008	January–May	August–December
2009	January–March	April–December
2010	March–October	November–December

Venus is the brightest object in the sky after the Sun and Moon. It appears as the "Evening Star" after sunset, or the "Morning Star" before sunrise.

Mars appears in the sky looking like a bright red star.

MARS

Mars is a rocky planet, half the diameter of Earth. It has a thin atmosphere of unbreathable carbon dioxide, and has no liquid water on its surface. The entire surface, apart from icy polar caps, is a dry, red desert. Mars has canyons and volcanoes larger than any on Earth. One volcano, Olympus Mons, is 25km (16 miles) high and 500km (315 miles) across. Mars has two small moons, Phobos and Deimos.

MARS – WHEN AND WHERE TO LOOK

YEAR	MONTHS VISIBLE	CONSTELLATION	PAGE
2006	January–February	Aries	18
	March–April	Taurus	21
	May	Gemini	20
	June	Cancer	15
2007	July	Aries	18
	August–September	Taurus	21
	October–December	Gemini	20
2008	January–March	Taurus	21
	April–May	Gemini	20
2009	August	Taurus	21
	September–October	Gemini	20
	November	Cancer	15
	December	Leo	15
2010	January	Leo	15
	February–May	Cancer	15

JUPITER

Jupiter is the largest planet in the Solar System. It spins faster than the Earth. On Jupiter, one day lasts less than 10 hours. The stripes visible through a telescope are cloud layers. Jupiter's most noticeable feature is the Great Red Spot. This is a huge storm that has been blowing for at least 300 years.

Jupiter appears as a bright yellowish-white point of light, brighter than any of the stars.

The Great Red Spot

JUPITER – WHEN AND WHERE TO LOOK

YEAR	MONTHS VISIBLE	CONSTELLATION	PAGE
2006	January–June	Libra	27
2007	January–July	Ophiuchus	17
2008	April–November	Sagittarius	27
2009	July–December	Capricornus	16
2010	August–December	Aquarius	19

41

For a link to a website about famous astronomers' ideas, turn to page 55.

SATURN

The second largest planet in the Solar System is Saturn. It consists almost entirely of substances that are gases on Earth: ammonia, methane, hydrogen and helium. Inside Saturn, enormous gravity compresses these into liquids.

Saturn is famous for its rings. These are made up of of billions of ice particles which orbit Saturn like miniature moons. Saturn has at least 34 moons. The largest, Titan, has orange clouds.

Saturn appears to the naked eye looking like a bright yellow star. Its rings are only visible through a telescope.

SATURN – WHEN AND WHERE TO LOOK

YEAR	MONTHS VISIBLE	CONSTELLATION	PAGE
2006	January–May	Cancer	15
	October–December	Leo	15
2007	January–May	Leo	15
	October–December	Leo	15
2008	January–May	Leo	15
	October–December	Leo	15
2009	January–April	Leo	15
	November–December	Virgo	14
2010	January–May	Virgo	14
	November–December	Virgo	14

URANUS, NEPTUNE, PLUTO

The three outer planets are not visible to the naked eye. Little was known about them until 1989, when the Voyager 2 spacecraft flew past Uranus and Neptune. It sent us detailed photographs of the planets and their rings and moons.

➡ URANUS
Discovered in 1781 by William Herschel. Uranus has at least 27 moons.

◄ NEPTUNE
Similar to Uranus in size. It has at least 13 moons. Its biggest moon, Triton is one of the largest satellites in the Solar System at 2,720km (1,700 miles) in diameter.

➡ PLUTO
Only very powerful telescopes can show Pluto and its large moon, Charon. Pluto's orbit passes inside Neptune's, so that between 1979 and1999, Neptune was the outermost planet.

Recently, astronomers have discovered very small planets, known as planetesimals, far beyond the orbit of Pluto. In future, this may mean that the number of planets in the Solar System changes.

COMETS

Comets are balls of ice, dust and rock. Some drift in huge orbits that extend far into space, even beyond the orbit of Pluto. As a comet nears the Sun, the heat turns the ice into a mini-atmosphere that streams out into a tail. One of the longest tails recorded was that of the Great Comet of 1843. It was about 330 million km (200 million miles) long. Sometimes a comet is large and bright enough to be seen without binoculars, but most are visible only through telescopes.

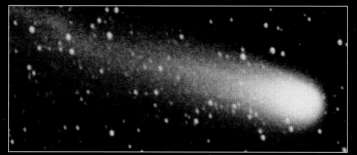

↑ HALLEY'S COMET
Of the comets that reappear regularly, the brightest is Halley's Comet, which reappears every 76 years. It will next appear sometime during 2061.

ASTEROIDS

Asteroids are large pieces of either rock, or rock and metal. Scientists believe they are bits and pieces that were left over when our Solar System formed. Many asteroids may measure over 100km (62 miles) across. However, only two (Vesta and Ceres) can be spotted with the naked eye.

Most asteroids orbit the Sun between Mars and Jupiter, in a region called the Asteroid Belt. Astronomers have recorded the orbits of about 4,000 asteroids, but they think there could be well over 10,000.

The distances between asteroids in the Asteroid Belt are huge. Spacecraft can pass through without hitting any of them.

DIAMETERS OF THE LARGEST ASTEROIDS

Ceres	932km (583 miles)
Vesta	538km (336 miles)
Pallas	522km (326 miles)
Hygeia	430km (269 miles)
Euphrosyne	370km (231 miles)

For a link to a website with asteroid and comet facts, turn to page 55.

THE MOON

The Moon is Earth's only natural satellite. It is 3,476km (2,172 miles) in diameter, which is about a quarter the diameter of Earth. The Moon's surface is covered with craters, up to 250km (150 miles) across. The craters were blasted out by asteroids and meteorites millions of years ago. The Moon also has mountains, some almost 10km (6.5 miles) high.

The dark patches which spread over large areas of the Moon are plains of solidified lava. Early astronomers thought they were seas and oceans, and they still have the Latin names "mare" (sea) and "oceanus" (ocean).

The Moon always keeps the same side facing Earth. It turns around completely in 27.3 days, exactly the same time as it takes to orbit the Earth.

This picture of the Moon shows some of the main lunar features which are easy to spot with unaided eyes.

Mare Imbrium
Sea of Showers

Copernicus
A crater

Oceanus Procellarum
Ocean of Storms

Mare Nubium
Sea of Clouds

Mare Humorum
Sea of Humours

Tycho
A crater

MARE TRANQUILLITATIS
Sea of Tranquility

MARE SERENITATIS
Sea of Serenity

MARE FECUNDITATIS
Sea of Fertility

MARE VAPORUM
Sea of Vapours

MARE HUMORUM
Sea of Humours

MARE IMBRIUM
Sea of Showers

MARE NECTARIS
Sea of Nectar

MARE CRISIUM
Sea of Crises

MARE NUBIUM
Sea of Clouds

MARE FRIGORIS
Sea of Cold

COPERNICUS
A crater

TYCHO
A crater

OCEANUS PROCELLARUM
Ocean of Storms

Mare Frigoris
Sea of Cold

Mare Serenitatis
Sea of Serenity

Mare Crisium
Sea of Crises

Mare Vaporum
Sea of Vapours

Mare Tranquillitatis
Sea of Tranquility

Mare Fecunditatis
Sea of Fertility

Mare Nectaris
Sea of Nectar

47

For a link to a site with virtual panoramas of the Moon, turn to page 54.

PHASES OF THE MOON

The Moon emits no light of its own. Like the planets, it just reflects sunlight. As the Moon orbits the Earth, different amounts of the sunlit half are visible, so the lit shape (called the phase) changes. The phases repeat every 29½ days.

This diagram shows how the Moon's phases occur.

Direction of sunlight

Moon

Earth

The pictures below show what the Moon looks like from Earth when it is in each of the numbered positions above.

1 New Moon **2** Crescent **3** Half Moon **4** Waxing

5 Full Moon **6** Waning **7** Half Moon **8** Crescent

THE MOON – FACTS AND FIGURES

Diameter	3,476km (2,172 miles)
Average distance from Earth	384,000km (240,250 miles)
Time taken to orbit Earth	27.3 days
Time to rotate once (lunar day)	27.3 days
Surface temperature by day	123°C (253°F)
Surface temperature by night	–123°C (–206°F)

ECLIPSES

⬅ ECLIPSE OF THE SUN

This occurs when the New Moon passes in front of the Sun, cutting off its light. In a total eclipse the Sun's corona (outer atmosphere) can be seen.

This diagram shows the Moon sliding over the face of the Sun during a total eclipse of the Sun.

➡ ECLIPSE OF THE MOON

This occurs when the Full Moon passes into the shadow of the Earth. There is little light to reflect, so the Moon dims and looks coppery-brown.

This diagram shows the Moon in the Earth's shadow during an eclipse of the Moon.

NEVER LOOK AT THE SUN

Never look at a solar eclipse, or view it through smoked glass, or through binoculars or a telescope. The Sun's rays may blind you. For how to watch an eclipse safely, go to **www.usborne-quicklinks.com**.

METEORS

Small pieces of debris floating around in the Solar System are called meteoroids. They range in size from enormous rocks to tiny grains of dust.

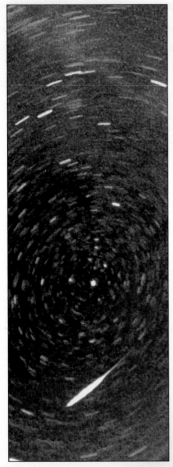

A photograph of a Perseid meteor shower (see the table on page 51)

METEORS
When meteoroids fall into the Earth's atmosphere, they burn up and make a bright streak across the sky. These are called meteors or shooting stars. On a clear night, you can see a few meteors every hour. A really bright meteor is called a fireball.

Fireball   Meteor

METEOR SHOWERS
Most small meteoroids are the remains of broken-up comets. When Earth passes through a stream of dust left by a comet, there are spectacular showers of meteors. You'll see dozens of meteors every hour. The table on the right gives information about when important meteor showers will occur.

METEORITES

Some meteors fall to the Earth as charred rocks. Once they hit the ground, these rocks are called meteorites. Look for them in museums.

⬆ STONY METEORITE

There are two main types of meteorites, stony and iron. Stony ones are called aerolites. They are often covered with a smooth black crust.

⬅ IRON METEORITE

Iron meteorites are also known as siderites. Examination under a microscope reveals a peculiar criss-cross pattern.

IMPORTANT METEOR SHOWERS

PEAK DATE	SHOWER NAME	FROM THE CONSTELLATION	NO. PER HOUR
Jan. 3/4*	Quadrantids	Left of Mizar/Alcor	up to 100
April 21	Lyrids	Lyra	up to 15
May 5	Eta Aquarids	Aquarius	up to 35
July 29	Delta Aquarids	Aquarius	up to 25
Aug. 12*	Perseids	Perseus	up to 80
Oct. 21	Orionids	Orion	up to 30
Nov. 17*	Leonids	Leo	variable
Dec. 13*	Geminids	Gemini	up to 100

Note: * indicates particularly good meteor showers.

51

For a link to a site where you can examine meteorites, turn to page 54.

OTHER SKY SIGHTS

In addition to planets and stars, there are other things to spot closer to the Earth.

↓ AURORA BOREALIS/ AUSTRALIS

This shimmering curtain effect is caused by radiation from the Sun striking particles in Earth's upper atmosphere. Known as the Borealis in the northern hemisphere and Australis in the southern hemisphere. The aurorae can usually be seen only from areas in the far north and the far south of the Earth.

← ZODIACAL LIGHT

A cone of light caused by sunlight reflecting off dust particles. The glow passes through the constellations of the zodiac. Best seen from tropics.

➡ HALO AROUND THE MOON

Caused by ice particles in the upper atmosphere. Usually only one silvery-white ring can be seen, but sometimes two.

For a link to a site where you can track satellites in 3D, turn to page 54.

ARTIFICIAL SATELLITES

Since the launch of Sputnik I in 1957, thousands of artificial satellites have been launched into orbit around the Earth. The largest ones can be seen with the naked eye. They look like slow, steadily moving points of silvery-white light. Beware of mistaking aircraft for satellites. Aircraft have red and blue identification lights on their wing-tips, and you can usually hear their engines on a quiet night.

TDRS Satellite

⬆ ARTIFICIAL SATELLITE

There are so many satellites that you will usually see one within an hour's spotting. As it passes into the Earth's shadow it will be eclipsed, fading out of sight. Some satellites flash because they are spinning in orbit. Sunlight reflects off different parts, causing a flashing effect.

Satellite

Flashing satellite

The International Space Station in orbit

⬅ SPACE STATIONS

Space stations orbit the Earth at a distance of about 400km (250 miles). They are laboratories where experiments can be done away from the effect of the Earth's gravity.

INTERNET LINKS

If you have access to the Internet, you can visit these websites to find out more about the night sky and space. For links to these sites, go to the Usborne Quicklinks Website at **www.usborne-quicklinks.com** and enter the keywords "spotters night sky".

Internet safety

When using the Internet, please follow the **Internet safety guidelines** shown on the Usborne Quicklinks Website.

WEBSITE 1 See the latest amazing pictures from the Hubble Space Telescope plus games and movies of the night sky.

WEBSITE 2 Visit the Moon, with virtual panoramas and some tricky lunar puzzles.

WEBSITE 3 A fun space website with lots of information, a quiz and ideas for space activities.

WEBSITE 4 Examine fragments of real meteorites online.

WEBSITE 5 Fly through a virtual Solar System and create its tenth planet.

WEBSITE 6 See a new astronomy picture every day, or browse the archives for photos of stunning night-sky objects.

WEBSITE 7 Track satellites around the world in 3D, including the ISS and the Hubble Space Telescope.

WEBSITE 8 Lots of information for amateur astronomers, including games, quizzes and an interactive star map.

WEBSITE 9 Watch space videos and animations, and track the International Space Station.

WEBSITE 10 Find out about the ideas of famous astronomers, from ancient times to today.

WEBSITE 11 Read about the latest space news and discoveries.

WEBSITE 12 Information about exploring the planets in our Solar System, as well as asteroids and comets, with facts about probes, landers and rovers.

You can find out about the latest launches on the Internet.

This amazing photograph was taken by the Hubble Space Telescope. It shows the Eagle Nebula, where many new stars are born.

TAKING PHOTOGRAPHS

You don't have to be an expert in photography to take some really good photos of the night sky.

SETTING UP YOUR CAMERA

You will need a single lens reflex (SLR) camera, which is a camera with a shutter that can be held open. Turn the focus ring until it is focused on infinity. Open the aperture to its widest setting – shown by the smallest "F" number.

To make sure the camera doesn't move when the picture is taken, place it on a wall or tripod. Ideally, you should use a shutter release cable to press the button.

Turn the focus ring until it is focused on infinity.

SLR camera

Open the aperture to its widest setting.

STAR TRAILS

Point your camera at any part of the sky. Keep the shutter open for at least ten minutes to get a result like the one shown here, as the stars rotate in the sky.

This picture shows star trails and an SLR camera, the best type of camera to take pictures of the night sky.

HANDY TIP

When you get your film processed, tell the assistant that the photos are of stars. Otherwise, it might be assumed that the results are mistakes and they may not be printed.

USEFUL WORDS

This glossary explains some of the terms used in this book. Words that appear in *italic* text are defined separately in the glossary.

asteroid – small rocky object orbiting the Sun. Thousands of them exist in the Asteroid Belt between Mars and Jupiter.

Big Bang – name given to the huge explosion that scientists think was the beginning of the Universe.

binary – two stars orbiting around each other.

eclipse – the total or partial blocking of one object in space by another. For example, in an eclipse of the Sun, the Sun is hidden by the Moon for a brief period.

galaxy – a giant group of stars. For example, the Milky Way galaxy contains about 100,000 stars.

hemisphere – half of a planet or moon. The top half is the northern hemisphere, the bottom half is the southern hemisphere.

Light Year – the distance light travels in a year. One light year (LY) is 9.46 million million* km (5.88 million million* miles).

meteor – a *meteoroid* that travels though Earth's atmosphere.

meteorite – a *meteoroid* that hits the Earth's suface.

meteoroid – a chunk of rock or dust flying in space.

nebula – cloud of dust and gas where new stars often form.

orbit – the path taken by one object as it revolves around another, for example, the planets orbit the Sun.

phases – different shapes that the moon and some planets seem to have as differing amounts of their sunlit sides are seen.

satellite – any object in space that orbits another object. Man-made satellites are launched into space to orbit the Earth.

star – a ball of constantly exploding gases, giving off light and heat.

sunspot – one of the dark patches that sometimes appear on the Sun.

white dwarf – tiny remains of a much larger star.

*Trillion in the USA

SCORECARD

After a night's spotting, write the date next to the objects you see in this scorecard. Keep a record of your nightly scores. The letter **N** or **S** next to an object indicates that it is visible only in the northern or southern hemisphere. Other objects, like meteorites, will usually be seen in museums, so score if you see them there.

	Score	Date spotted		Score	Date spotted
Aurora Australis (**S**)	35		Canes Venatici (**N**)	15	
Aurora Borealis (**N**)	35		Canis major	5	
Zodiacal light	40		Canis minor	10	
Artificial satellites Flashing satellite	15		Capricornus	15	
Satellite	5		Carina (**S**)	10	
Constellations Andromeda	5		Cassiopeia (**N**)	5	
Antlia (**S**)	15		Centaurus (**S**)	5	
Apus (**S**)	10		Cepheus (**N**)	10	
Aquarius	10		Cetus (**N**)	15	
Aquila	5		Chameleon (**S**)	20	
Ara (**S**)	15		Circinus (**S**)	20	
Aries	10		Columba (**S**)	15	
Auriga	5		Coma Berenices	15	
Boötes	5		Corona Australis (**S**)	10	
Caelum (**S**)	20		Corona Borealis	10	
Camelopardalis (**N**)	20		Corvus	10	
Cancer	10		Crater	15	

	Score	Date spotted		Score	Date spotted
Crux (S)	5		Monoceros	20	
Cygnus	5		Musca (S)	15	
Delphinus	10		Norma (S)	20	
Dorado (S)	15		Octans (S)	20	
Draco (S)	10		Ophiuchus	10	
Equuleus	20		Orion	5	
Eridanus	10		Pavo (S)	15	
Fornax (S)	20		Pegasus	5	
Gemini	5		Perseus (N)	10	
Grus (S)	15		Phoenix (S)	15	
Hercules	10		Pictor (S)	20	
Horologium (S)	15		Pisces	15	
Hydra (S)	15		Piscis Austrinus	15	
Hydrus (S)	15		Puppis	15	
Indus (S)	15		Pyxis (S)	20	
Lacerta (N)	15		Reticulum (S)	15	
Leo	5		Sagitta	15	
Leo minor (N)	15		Sagittarius	5	
Lepus	10		Scorpius	5	
Libra	15		Sculptor (S)	20	
Lupus (S)	15		Scutum	15	
Lynx (N)	15		Serpens	15	
Lyra	5		Sextans	20	
Mensa (S)	20		Taurus	5	
Microscopium (S)	20		Telescopium (S)	15	

	Score	Date spotted		Score	Date spotted
Triangulum	15		Mare Fecunditatis	15	
Triangulum Australe (S)	10		Mare Frigoris	15	
Tucana (S)	15		Mare Humorum	15	
Ursa major (N)	5		Mare Imbrium	10	
Ursa minor (N)	10		Mare Nectaris	15	
Vela	10		Mare Nubium	15	
Virgo	10		Mare Serenitatis	10	
Volans (S)	20		Mare Tranquillitatis	10	
Vulpecula	15		Mare Vaporum	15	
Eclipses: Lunar Partial	30		Oceanus Procellarum	5	
Total	40		Copernicus	10	
Eclipses: Solar Partial	50		Tycho	10	
Total	100		**Phases of the moon** New Moon	5	
Meteors Fireball	30		Crescent	5	
Meteor	20		Half Moon	5	
Iron meteorite	30		Waxing	5	
Stony meteorite	30		Full Moon	5	
Meteor showers Eta Aquarids	30		Waning	5	
Geminids	30		Halo around the Moon	15	
Lyrids	20		**Nebulae and star clusters**		
Orionids	25		Horse's Head Nebula	80	
Perseids	15		Lagoon Nebula	20	
Quadrantids	20		Orion Nebula	10	
Taurids	20		Pleiades (N)	10	
Moon Mare Crisium	10		Praesepe	15	

	Score	Date spotted		Score	Date spotted
Planets Jupiter	10		Andromeda Galaxy	15	
Mars	10		Antares	5	
Mercury	15		Betelgeuse	5	
Saturn	15		Magellanic Cloud (**S**)	10	
Uranus	20		Milky Way	5	
Venus	10		Mira	15	
Stars and galaxies Alcor (**N**)	10		Mizar (**N**)	5	
Algol (**N**)	20		Sirius	5	

NOTES

INDEX

ACKNOWLEDGEMENTS

The publisher would like to thank the
following individuals and organizations:
Illustrations: Gary Bines and Kuo Kang Chen
p10-13 star maps by Karen Webb
Photographs: cover © Digital Vision
1 © Getty Images/Johnny Johnson; 2–3 © Royalty-
Free/CORBIS; 4–5 Digital Vision; 8 (Sun) with thanks to
NASA; 28 (Lagoon Nebula) with thanks to NASA; (Praesepe) © by 1998
Wil Milan (http://www.astrophotographer.com/); 29 (Orion Nebula) Digital Vision;
(Pleiades) D.F. Malin © Royal Observatory, Edinburgh/ AATB; 33 (Antares) Royal
Observatory Edinburgh/ Science Photo Library, (Betelgeuse) with thanks to
NASA; 34 (Horse's Head Nebula) NASA, (Milky Way) Fred Espenak/DODD/ Science
Photo Library; 35 (Andromeda Galaxy, Large Magellanic Clouds) Digital Vision;
(Small Magellanic Clouds) Celestial Image Co./ Science Photo Library; 38 US
Geological Survey/ Science Photo Library; 36–37 Digital Vision; 39 Digital Vision;
40 Digital Vision; 41 Digital Vision; 42 Digital Vision; 43 (Neptune and Uranus)
Digital Vision; 44 Digital Vision; 50 (Meteor shower) © V. Winter (ICSTARS.COM);
51 (iron meteorite) by Carl Allen/ with thanks to NASA, (stony meteorite) by
Cecilia Satterwhite/ with thanks to NASA; 52 (Aurora Borealis) David Pettitt;
(Zodiacal light) © Roger Ressmeyer/Corbis (Halo around the Moon) © Dennis di
Cicco/Corbis; 53 (ISS) with thanks to NASA; 54 (Eagle Nebula and Shuttle take-
off) © Digital Vision; 56-57 (photo and backgrounds) Stuart Atkinson
Backgrounds: 6–13, 28–29, 38–43, 46–47, 58–64 Digital Vision